THIS BLOOMSBURY BOOK

BELONGS TO

....

BLOOMSBURY
CHILDREN'S
BOOKS

For my mother with all my heart – H.W.

For Anni, Samu and Sara – A.S.

Far, far in the North, where the first snow falls even in summertime, a special village is hidden away – the village where Santa and all his Helpers dwell. And there lived a little Helper who couldn't wait for Christmas.

He was always the first to bring a Christmas tree back from the great forest, and first to clean his sleigh, polish his boots and spruce up his red Christmas coat.

As for presents, the little Helper had his wrapped and ready while the other Helpers were still choosing theirs.
He liked to give toys that he had made himself. He could make all sorts of things, like brightly-coloured cars, spotted wooden dogs, rocking horses and dolls' houses.

He also baked wonderful cinnamon stars, honey cakes and chocolate cookies, while his gingerbread was the finest in the whole world.

Once all the presents were wrapped and biscuits baked, he looked forward to delivering them to the children more than any other Helper – but every year the same thing happened . . .

'No, you can't come,' said the Chief Helper, who was in charge of everything in the village. 'You are too small.'
'The children would laugh their heads off!' shouted one cheeky young Helper. 'If they could even see him,' laughed another. 'With his micro-sleigh!' mocked a third. They were being very mean, and the Chief Helper would have liked to leave them behind too.

But this year there were so many presents to deliver that he needed everyone. So instead he gave them a stern look, and said to the littlest Helper, 'Perhaps next year.' But the little Helper was beginning to doubt it.

He didn't want to see or hear the other Helpers set off on their journey with Santa, so he closed the shutters and stayed in his room all alone.

He didn't mind that he was smaller than the others, but he was very sad that he wasn't allowed to go and visit the children.

In the evening, when everything lay quiet and deserted, he ventured outside. He wasn't allowed to fly with the others, but he could at least stretch his legs. The stars twinkled, but the little Helper didn't look at them. The others would be flying up there somewhere in their reindeer sleigh ... Then suddenly he heard voices in the great forest. Only the animals lived in the forest. What were they talking about so late at night?

The little Helper was small
enough to sneak up close without
the animals noticing him. The
squirrel was there and the hare, the
bear, the wild pig and the mice …
And they were all complaining.
'It's not fair,' growled the bear. 'Santa and his Helpers take
presents to humans every year, but they never come to us animals.'
'And we're right on their doorstep,' grumbled the hare.
'It's always been like that,' sighed the old owl. 'I'm afraid it will
never change.'

But it did change! As soon as the little Helper heard what the animals were saying, he silently slipped away and ran home. He checked his clothes in the mirror, packed the presents on to an old sleigh, and then he was off again. He had no reindeer as they had all gone with the other Helpers, but he could easily push the sleigh as far as the forest.

That evening the animals had a party. The great forest had never seen anything like it. All the animals received presents, but the growly bear was happiest of all – he had never been given anything in his life before. And the owl was proudest – she tried on her new pullover and was instantly the best-dressed bird in the whole forest.

As soon as the other Helpers returned, the little Helper went to the Chief and told him what had happened. The Chief Helper was amazed and appointed him 'Santa for the Animals'.
'Bravo!' shouted the others, and carried him high on their shoulders. And ever since then the little Helper has been just as important as the big ones.

Every

single

year.